THE
FERRYBOAT RIDE

ROBERT PERRY

ILLUSTRATIONS BY GRETA GUZEK

NIGHTWOOD

All Aboard!

Two by two
The cars now park,
Like animals
For Noah's ark!

We're Off!

They raise the ramp,
They close the doors;
The engine rumbles!
The engine roars!

Who Is Moving?

All of a sudden
We're in the bay—
Is that the land
Floating away?

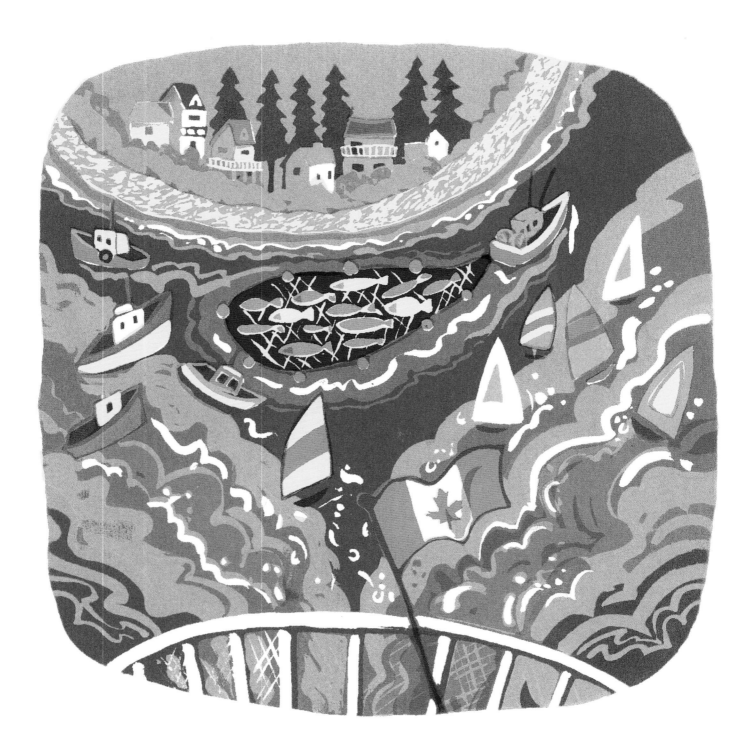

In the Wake

The waves are foaming!
Perhaps they mind
That they are left
So far behind?

The Seagulls

Look at the seagulls
Enjoying the cruise,
Racing the ferry,
Pretending to lose!

Windy

Be sure to grab
The nearest pole:
The ferryboat
Plays rock-'n'-roll!

Through Active Pass

We're coming through!
The narrows nears.
The whistle blows!
We clap our ears!

The Lighthouse

By day it gleams
Bright red and white,
Then flashes gold
All through the night.

Watercolours

The ocean sparkles
In paintbox blues,
Cloud-speckled skies
In purple hues.

The Whales

Do you believe
In ferry tales
Of seeing pods
Of flying whales?

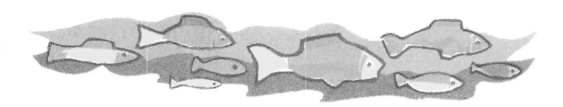

Tug of War

A tiny tugboat,
A giant barge:
Which will win...
The small or the large?

On Shore Again

Toward the dock
We quickly float;
Let's say goodbye
To the ferryboat!

NIGHTWOOD EDITIONS,
RR2, S26 C13,
Gibsons, BC Canada V0N 1V0

Design by Greta Guzek and Roger Handling

Canadian Cataloguing in Publication Data

Perry, Robert, 1951-
The Ferryboat Ride

Poems.
ISBN 0-88971-155-0

I. Guzek, Greta. II. Title.
PS8581.E77F4 1993 jC811'.54 C93-091160-1
PZ8.3.P47Fe 1993

Printed in Canada